The Beasts
of Lake Oph

NewCon Press Novellas

Set 1: Science Fiction (Cover art by Chris Moore)
    The Iron Tactician – Alastair Reynolds
    At the Speed of Light – Simon Morden
    The Enclave – Anne Charnock
    The Memoirist – Neil Williamson

Set 2: Dark Thrillers (Cover art by Vincent Sammy)
    Sherlock Holmes: Case of the Bedevilled Poet – Simon Clark
    Cottingley – Alison Littlewood
    The Body in the Woods – Sarah Lotz
    The Wind – Jay Caselberg

Set 3: The Martian Quartet (Cover art by Jim Burns)
    The Martian Job – Jaine Fenn
    Sherlock Holmes: The Martian Simulacra – Eric Brown
    Phosphorous: A Winterstrike Story – Liz Williams
    The Greatest Story Ever Told – Una McCormack

Set 4: Strange Tales (Cover art by Ben Baldwin)
    Ghost Frequencies – Gary Gibson
    The Lake Boy – Adam Roberts
    Matryoshka – Ricardo Pinto
    The Land of Somewhere Safe – Hal Duncan

Set 5: The Alien Among Us (Cover art by Peter Hollinghurst)
    Nomads – Dave Hutchinson
    Morpho – Philip Palmer
    The Man Who Would be Kling – Adam Roberts
    Macsen Against the Jugger – Simon Morden

Set 6: Blood and Blade (Cover art by Duncan Kay)
    The Bone Shaker – Edward Cox
    A Hazardous Engagement – Gaie Sebold
    Serpent Rose – Kari Sperring
    Chivalry – Gavin Smith

Set 7: Robot Dreams (Cover art by Fangorn)
    According To Kovac – Andrew Bannister
    Deep Learning – Ren Warom
    Paper Hearts – Justina Robson
    The Beasts Of Lake Oph – Tom Toner

The Beasts
of Lake Oph

Tom Toner

NewCon Press
England

First published in the UK by NewCon Press
41 Wheatsheaf Road, Alconbury Weston, Cambs, PE28 4LF
March 2020

NCP229 (limited edition hardback)
NCP230 (softback)

10 9 8 7 6 5 4 3 2 1

ISBN:

978-1-912950-54-6 (hardback)
978-1-912950-55-3 (softback)

Cover art by Fangorn
Cover layout by Ian Whates

Minor Editorial meddling by Ian Whates
Final Text layout by Storm Constantine

One

There wasn't much point in going underground; that wasn't how the bomb worked. All they could hope for was some last-minute reprieve.

Henrietta watched the sky beyond the window, a blush of evening creeping across the city, her pixel eye jiggling back and forth and up and down to compensate for the trembling of the woman she clung to, so that the image lay perfectly still. And then she saw it.

Two

Bluish light and grey mud and the wittering of the Slaughterwoods on either bank of the river, the slop of water against the hull waking him fully. Roh dithered in the boat with his great legs pulled up to his chin, arranging his baggage and passing it to the Tallfolk on the bank, in no hurry. He had slept that way, and now uncurled stiffly, accepting some guiding spindly hands that he almost crushed with his own as he stumbled onto the wooden jetty. He stretched, yawning mightily and spraying a gust of spittle from between the spines of his whiskers, gazing at the towering woods on the far bank and the cleared, weedy path that lay before him, hoisting his pack around his neck for the trudge.

It was a fair hike to the lakeshore, the virgin forest only recently cleared. They moved in silence but for the reedy music of the Tallfolk up ahead, something to dispel the fear. Roh could understand, and peered around him with small dark eyes, his spots dimming, the light shrinking to a dawn pallor as they passed deeper into the forest.

The Slaughterwoods were a murk of scent and sound: the *pip-pip* of a Vurret as it called for mates in the bowers of a Gigmur tree, rattling screeches of a colony of red Chacels, the *uyum! uyum!* cries of a hunting Yeen. And the flora itself, fatty stands of toothy Yelphus, a towering, be-fingered Thummi ready to snatch anything that tickled its dangling feelers, the tongue leaves of a Thralgul drooling in anticipation. The Tallfolk would have endured stings and scrapes and rashes beyond thinking, their hardwood blades blunted by months of hacking and slashing and burning. Roh had heard that some had gone missing in these carnivorous woods; there were things, undocumented creatures, the stuff of local myths.

It had all begun three hundred seasons ago, when Strongfolk industry delved deeper into the crust of the world than ever before, and the first of the large pre-Luphri tunnels had been found.

What had made the tunnels was anyone's guess – and everything from great worms to clever Mimaks had been suggested – but two generations of fearless explorers had braved the depths to map them, discovering that they coiled right around the planet. It was clear from the outset that they were not a geological phenomenon, firstly due to the mathematical precision of their dimensions, and secondly because testing of the smooth walls revealed that they had once been lined entirely with Gleam.

Gleam. A treasure beyond imagining, so rare that only a few small grains were ever in circulation at any one time. Harder than Echowood, sharper than a Jhorral's tooth, smooth and glassy to the touch.

It was not until the last regime that the Ghipheth tunnels – named for their discoverer, a Tallfolk miner who died mere days later in a cave-in – could be accurately light-aged, producing a number that fired even the most practical Strongfolk's imagination: the tunnels were one hundred and forty thousand ages old. Older than almost anything discovered, save for the horrifying Mimaks a few geological layers below.

One hundred and forty thousand ages, or two hundred and fifty eight million seasons, as Roh preferred to think of it. A gulf of dizzying vertigo, of such time beneath their feet.

'You all right back there?' called Braldron, the leading Tall One, in his expressive language. 'It's not far now.' His soft crimson beak opened up like a flower as he spoke, a glimpse of black tongue darting around inside.

Roh raised a hand and fluttered his spots, puffing a little at the steepening incline and removing his broad-brimmed wooden hat, sticky and stinking beneath his Mun-wool shawl. He'd never visited the Ophiphi lake system – the lowlands had been off limits due to a series of civil conflicts that had eventually sparked a war that still raged further west – but he understood from the great shells and colourstone deposits that lined the land that this part of the world must have lain underwater for some considerable time. The buried creatures had stayed hidden until some upheaval in the past – perhaps when the Strongfolk were still aquatic leviathans themselves – had pushed everything into the light.

And with it what had once been rumours, rumours of cave-like chambers in the rock, of curious little fossils the likes of which had never been seen before.

They came to the cliff's edge, the light brightening through the woods. Roh squinted, sweating, as he stood alongside the party of Tallfolk, surveying the great broken blue expanse of Ophipi, the line of its wooden dam, and the distant, cloud-wreathed mountains beyond.

'The cliff's crumbling badly,' said Braldron, tall and stooped and spindly beside him, and Roh glanced at the weeds and stone beneath his boots.

'We've been working to prop it,' Braldron continued, leading them to a signposted path that wound back through the trees and down to a flight of steps cut into the cliff. Roh noticed that in one long-fingered hand he held a wooden paddle gun. 'But all this undermining's going to bring it down, eventually.'

Roh considered this as he came to the steps. 'So, the lake will be the only way out?' he asked Braldron in his clumsy approximation of their language. He'd been told it sounded to them like children-speak. 'I'm supposed to be here all winter.'

Braldron's beady yellow and green-flecked eyes remained fixed on the stone steps beneath his feet. 'Cliff comes down when it likes – I'm sure they'll lay on barges after that.'

They descended from the lip of the cliff, a tangy, stagnant wind reaching them from the lake, stepping past a series of echowood beams that rose beside the rocky stairway and into the undercut above. Roh saw the first Strong workers further below, their backs gleaming bronze, and beyond them the makeshift cone settlement at the lakehead.

Braldron had paused up ahead to speak to some of the miners, and was busily gesticulating to the cliff face. Roh took the opportunity to glance once more back the way they'd come, conscious that every step he took down the hill's cut face dropped him past a deeper layer of time. He estimated that in their current position they were something like a hundred million seasons deep, enough time for the world, the Everywhere, to have been quite unrecognisable. Everything from creatures and plant life to the very shapes of the lands themselves must have been different back then, when Roh's ancestors – they knew – had swum in the seas, and Braldron's had glided through the air. Such palpable eternity, all around them: lives and worlds they'd never dreamed existed.

They reached the bottom not long before midday, panting beneath the winter sun. Roh dumped his bags with some of the Tallfolk and headed for the largest of the cone dwellings, a colourful, peaked house of thorny turrets rising from the middle of the camp.

'Emai Icai Roh!'

Roh turned at the clumsy pronunciation of his name. A

stooped, wrinkly creature, unclothed but for a pinkish hair scarf that dangled with pouches and tools, was ambling his way. Her blonde whiskers were almost long enough to brush the ground. It was a small female Commoner – a cousin species – her spots flickering as soon as they made eye contact to produce a perfect version of his name, and hers.

Emai Phig Hassoh, director.

They matched their spot colours in a formal greeting, the director lapsing back into Tallspeak for the benefit of the others grouped behind her.

'You'll have met Unph Braldron, the excavator,' she said, indicating the emaciated stick of a creature to her left, who had accompanied him. 'These are Ingaeth and Luno, joint chief preparators.'

Roh bent quickly and touched his whiskers to their segmented beaks, smelling the Rassus spirit on them. By his reckoning it was the end of work, despite it being only midday, and threads of smoke were already rising from the peaks of the surrounding cones, the cooking fires lit. He had two whole nights to catch up with everything before starting at the site.

'You came up from Zulzer?' the director asked as they strode towards the primary cone.

Roh produced a brief tut of his tongue to indicate the affirmative. 'Through the monsoons. Seeing the sun again was a relief.'

'Well it's only going to get hotter,' she replied, her mind seemingly far away as she gazed at the works along the shoreline. 'We've already started moving the settlement backwards in case the cliff comes down. Only the operations cone will stay where it is, for now.' Hassoh squinted at the sun, brilliant overhead. 'So. We can either get you caught up in two, or I can take you for a quick look at the beasts before dinner. Your choice.'

Roh laughed, a squeaky set of inhalations. 'I haven't come all this way to go to bed, director.'

'Good.'

They turned towards the operations cone, the large and colourful dwelling Roh had seen on his way in. The two-storey building was a stiff teepee of moulded colourstone towers, its surface a swirl of oily tones, sunbleached at its spires. A temporary site dwelling: when they were done with it the place would be cleared and the chambers dismantled, industrial furnaces switched on to melt the cone and its turrets down to a flat disk, which was then barged back across the lake.

Roh and the director passed through a bustle of activity at its entrance; Tallfolk coming and going, locking up their work for the twicenight, fetching their friends for dinner. They paused at the sight of the director, repeating her name as she passed, their green-eyed gazes sliding over Roh, the newest arrival.

The place seemed larger inside, the light, which passed through the cone in a ruby-green blend, colouring everything. Roh's attention was drawn immediately to the six slabs of sooty rock arranged in wooden cases along the curved wall, each only one third of his size. Forgetting himself, he quickened his pace to get a better look.

They had been small. Shorter than a Commoner, lighter and more wiry than the Tallfolk. The narrow-boned fossils were squashed as thin as paper, a delicate tracery of brittle limbs and ribs and contorted, knobbly spines, patterned in shades of umber and russet.

Roh peered at what must have been a skull, at the expressive open holes of its eye sockets, the peg teeth yawning in a silent scream.

Were they crushed? he asked, lapsing back into Spotspeak, not turning to her. He knew from his reading that the creatures' bones were quite different from their own – solid, rigid things that could snap and shatter. It sounded to Roh like the most revolting, unnecessary suffering.

We don't know for sure. Hassoh came alongside. *It must have been something sudden.*

11

Roh looked closer, his face mere inches away. A hint of something diaphanous surrounded the fossil he studied, like a flowing skin pressed lightly into the stone. *Is that a flesh imprint?*

Director Hassoh touched it with her finger, following the line of the slight indentation. Roh did the same. *Probably.* She glanced at him. *Want to see the mock ups?*

Roh's eyes widened, his spots glowed. He tutted a yes.

They went through to a side room still occupied by whispering Tallfolk, the sounds of their muttering amplified in the vaulted space. There they were.

Half a dozen peculiar yellow forms stood in their midst, raised on small tables. They had been built from Zuzzwax and wooden poles, a fresh guesswork of musculature and skin applied that morning.

'Our best estimate,' said Hassoh in Tall, running her hand across the still-warm surface of the nearest form.

Roh stroked his whiskers, stepping closer. They were unlike any animal alive. Over the hint of one skull drooped folded sags of skin – what he'd seen imprinted around the fossils, so that they looked clothed in eerie shrouds. Between the first sculpture's scrawny arms the flesh was tight and wing-like (so perhaps they could *fly*, he thought, narrowing his eyes), and their feet were heavy and woolen, capped with hooves.

His eyes met those of the wax figure. Pure guesswork had been used here, and a pair of wide, slitted red pupils stared back at him. It was like something out of a bad dream, evolved during a time when the sun was dimmer, they thought.

A dim landscape, so strange and horrible.

'The others are rather wilder, more for fun,' said Hassoh, and Roh went over to gaze at the remaining figures. Some were entirely winged, others equipped with fins and a long tail. One was twice the size and all fluff, like a Rinki, the eyes so deep-set that they peered out from deep, furred holes in its head, and positioned so that it walked on all fours.

'The jaws had a bite force much greater than ours,' Hassoh continued, 'but the back teeth were made for chewing – see how flattened they are?'

Roh, supposedly the resident tooth-specialist, leaned in to see inside one of the mannequin's mouths, scenting pungent wax. He didn't like the sharp fangs at the front.

'The family tree,' he said slowly, twirling his whiskers. 'They're not Mimaks?'

'No. Seventy or eighty million seasons between the two, at the very least.'

Roh thought about this. 'So what did they become? What are they now?'

'Who knows? Their bones bear a slight similarity to the Luphri and the Lupherra – it's possible the beasts were their gigantic ancestors. Excavator Ilat even suggested they aren't from this world at all.'

Roh stared at her, his guts fluttering at the thought.

Hassoh clapped her hands together. 'Catch up on your rest, it will all be here in three days' time.'

Roh took dinner with the director and her Tallfolk preparators – dishes of egg paste and raw spineshells from the lake – before going to the small cone assigned to him for the twicenight.

Strongfolk (and Tallfolk, to a lesser degree) slept for two whole days and nights, rose for one and then repeated the process. Roh, though he was already caught up on his sleep from the journey and not remotely tired, was required to fall into sync with the rest of the camp, and work would not resume for another three days.

Silence descended. The last stragglers went off to their cones, the day still bright. Roh watched from his little circular window, listening to the warble of the woods while he peered out at the shores of the lake. They had problems with a predator here, the boatpeople had told him – someone snatched away in the last twicenight, footprints discovered that wound all the way through the camp. Roh went and locked his door, the still air cool inside his compartment, and opened up his bags. Strongfolk lived a mostly silent life (communicating with their iridescent spots, which glowed brightly in blues and greens in the twilight so that you could communicate with varying degrees of success over great distances); all this noise and talk had been stressful, and the garrulous Tallfolk were already grating on his nerves. He made a mental note not to talk too much of their gibberish-speak in future, not to encourage them.

Roh unpacked his toiletries, a set of brushes and scrapers and jugs, and set them beside his bed pole: a crooked wooden stick padded at its tip. Because of their posture, his people could not lie down – and were rarely able to get up again without assistance if they fell – so they slept leaning on a pole, their heavy calf muscles locked. Next he took out his puzzler, checking it carefully to make sure it hadn't been damaged in transit. The wooden computer click-clacked into life, mechanisms snicking back and forth inside, a ream of paper chugging around the spindle as the first colour-dot message appeared.

That director, too, might cause problems. He hadn't been prepared for someone so hands on. He would need to take care.

When Roh was done with his puzzler the light had nearly faded. He'd heard a Tall One's soft, quick footsteps making their way out to the slurry pit, and looked out to see the avian form strutting through the gloom, lantern held high, then nothing else. He slid the catch on the machine, opening it up and removing all the printed pieces of coloured paper, which he placed carefully into the fire, stirring the ashes. At full dark he would go outside, take a look.

Three

The moon, glowing through the tangled woods, struck him like a slap as he left his chamber. Roh squinted at it – with any luck it would sink below the hill. The world, the *Everywhere*, was still a dangerous place, and he kept a small wooden paddle and some stones on his person as he moved between the conical huts, keeping his footfalls light. Director Hassoh had ordered a moat dug around the camp after the Commoner was taken, but it hadn't been started yet, and their camp was still open to the Slaughter woods. Roh kept to the shadows, watchful.

There. Eye shine. Roh froze, his spots darkening in fear.

The glint vanished, accompanied by a frenzied pattering. A Luphri, an armless, bipedal primate the size of Roh's hand, rummaging around the slurry pits with its toes. The smell wafted on the night air in his direction. They were nasty little bitey things, the Luphri, but were no danger to something his size. And if they were out and about, it probably meant the coast was clear.

Roh looked to the central square, where a few lights burned. There didn't seem to be a night watch. Another stroke of luck. Roh's spots glimmered: perhaps he'd be done sooner than expected.

The cliff towered above the camp, striped light and dark in

the moonlight. Even from a distance Roh could make out the charcoal grey layer of the dig site beneath paler bands of chalk and shell and colourstone, a frenzy of ladders and platforms connecting it to the black mouths of caves below. Roh glanced behind him once more, quite sure he could explain himself if caught, and advanced upon the cliff face.

The beasts' layer was squashed sideways, running aslant up the cliff face in a wandering line of grey. Roh reached the top of the ladder and carefully negotiated the wooden platform, the assemblage wobbling under his weight. He froze as the pulleys squeaked, the night air cool so high above the lakebed, and glanced past his foot at the great drop beneath. The director was up here every day, and, though she wasn't nearly as heavy as Roh, she must have brought other Strongfolk up here. He shifted his foot, waiting to hear the crack, and gripped the pulley, eventually tearing his gaze from the drop.

They had cut into the cliff face, chiselling the soft layers of stone and digging down into the seam. Roh waited until he was off the wooden platform and standing on the rock, letting the moonlight guide his tentative steps, and then he began to hum. The soundless tune did not come from his mouth, but was instead a song of the spots, the colourful speckles on his flanks and arms glowing into faint life, lighting up the pulverized landscape of stone around him. He stared.

Glistening trenches extended into the cut slope, and the black holes of tunnels dug into the depths of the cliff face.

This is why it's falling down, he thought, stepping into the labyrinth of pits. *They've dug too far.*

He surveyed the scene for a moment longer, checking once more that he wasn't visible to the camp below, and stepped onto the first of the Thrisselwood planks laid throughout the site. It squeaked beneath his feet, loud and angry in the darkness, a pattering of crumbled shale loosed and slipping. It was hardly safe, people must have fallen. But then Roh saw the rope ahead, and grabbed it.

The first graves, cut into the wall: empty rectangles where fossils had been found last season. Roh peered into them before moving on, deeper. Here there were little makeshift lean-tos and equipment, a puzzler left carelessly out. Roh inspected it, reading some pages in the soft, cast light of his spots, and moved on. The field of death was vast, a plateau of hidden treasure unglimpsed from the camp – he would need to feign surprise and awe when Hassoh brought him up here again, but right now he needn't pretend. It was extraordinary.

Amongst the lines of rope enclosures there must have been layers of fossils hundreds deep, an ecosystem of beings suddenly extinguished. The violence that had been done to them implied something more than a burial, he had read, and as Roh looked down between his feet he saw a claw-like mass of clutching hand bones crushed into the exposed rock.

Small hands. Five fingers. They could hardly have been as dexterous as the Strongfolk, or as nimble as the eleven-fingered Tall, whose hands were as long as Roh's arm. Perhaps the beasts were household pets, left behind by something as yet unseen, to suffer this natural disaster alone.

He stood and surveyed the silence of this mass grave, the moon bathing it in stark gloss and glimmer, as if it were still putrid and wet with rot. By the moon's light he could make out the impression of regularity in the stone, a crumpled hive of regular spaces. The traces left of their dwellings. Roh squatted, rubbing at the demarcation of a boundary wall. It was nothing but a mark in the rock, as if a substance had flowed and moulded into the spaces, leaving only an impression.

There were six tunnels, bored at regular intervals into the cliff face. Roh knew they led all the way down beneath the woods and below the level of the lake, while above, in the rough-hewn rocks of the cliff top, a messy tangle of woodland and scrub dangled down. Roh saw how this inefficient mine worked at last – they couldn't have dug straight down without clearing the top back, and such a task would take months, even with slashing and burning. He wondered how far they'd get before the whole thing came down around them. How much warning would they have? That couldn't be his concern. He needed them to dig as fast as they could, to scoop as much as they could. He crouched, entering the dark tunnel mouth, the moonlight ending at a line just inside.

Roh breathed in the still darkness, his heart racing, and let his spots glow. Multicoloured light lit up the tunnel, its roughly scraped walls stretching down at an incline into the gloom. Inside he knew there were chambers, even living spaces, where more of the tomb had been exposed.

'Anyone there?' he called softly in Tallspeak, moving on when only an echo of his clumsy, scratchy voice spoke back to him. Spirits abounded in the myths of the Everywhere, but they came from the stars, not the dead. The dead were but broken machines.

Deeper, and he saw that shelves had been built into the rock, flat wooden spaces for the Tall to rest and the Strong to store their tools. A specially levelled water road, fitted with locks to raise its goods up the tiered sections of tunnel, had been dug into the stone for a small, uncrewed wooden raft connected to a rope pull, shipping tools in, fossils out. Roh rested an arm on one of the shelves, wrinkling his nose at the musk of the tunnel, and decided he'd gone deep enough that night.

The moon had sunk by the time he reached the base of the cliff, and the lake was nothing but a great absence of light, only the twinkling line of the dam and its tiny port hinting at any world beyond the camp.

Four

A gentle tapping woke him, sluggish and dazed, from a dream of the map he held in his hands. Roh stumbled as he left the lean stick, wiping a line of drool from his whiskers as he attempted to fix the topography of the map in his mind, but it was gone.

He washed and brushed his leathery skin, oiling the auburn wrinkles of his back with Zuzzcream and sipping a cup of Rassus while he glanced around his hovel, making sure everything was locked away, then made for the central cone.

'We had some new arrivals in the night,' Hassoh said in Tallspeak, standing before the collection of preparators and experts. Roh twisted on his leaning staff to glance at the people in question, a couple of Strongfolk and a Commoner.

The director indicated the Commoner, a spotted umber female considerably smaller than herself. 'Please welcome Emai Qah, archivist, and her team of Memorists from –' Hassoh hesitated and glanced at her spot sheet, little eyes searching.

'Downway,' said one of the Strongfolk. He flattened the hump of his neck in a gesture of humility, spots dulled almost to nothing, and pointed to himself and the larger brute beside him. 'Ong and Tang. We'll be recording the dig from here on out.'

Roh felt his spots flicker. Nobody had told him there'd be Memorists here. He flattened the muscles of his neck a little as he caught Tang's eye, turning back to the director.

'So.' Her eyes flicked to her assistant and he dragged in one of the wax model specimens. 'We know that where the Ophiphi hills now stand there was once – millions of seasons ago – a large inland sea. It covered the land from here all the way to the Chomm mountains, and settled atop the ruins of what appears to be a previously unknown society of sentient beings.' She flicked her gaze to the winged, red-eyed wax model of the Oph beast. 'We know they were clever, because they built things, just like us,' (at this point Roh turned to his spot sheets, skimming along to the printed drawings of the map of the dig site) 'and that the remnants of these dwellings have been preserved with them in the mudstone.'

At this point a Tall One walked amongst them, dishing out small lumps of charcoal-coloured rock to the newcomers. Roh took a piece and turned it in his hands. It was crumbly and fine-grained. He lifted it to his insensitive nostrils and took a long, hard sniff, detecting the faintest whiff of something sour.

'Precisely what this mudstone is composed of remains a mystery – tasters say it resembles melted colourstone – but it has been speculated that it is the one physical remnant of whatever caused the cataclysm that buried the creatures and their society. A sort of ash, perhaps, or sand.' She let them sniff the pieces of rock some more before continuing. 'It does not appear in any other rock strata in the country, or, as far as we know, elsewhere.'

She paused as the Tall One collected the rocks from everyone, before moving to a wooden board painted with large blue dot writing of every shade, a timeline of the region. Roh peered at it from the middle of the group, trying to see over the head of one of the preparators. Most of the Tallfolk could read Spot if required, but for their benefit there was a second board

scribbled all over with their own curious writing. It looked to
Roh like nothing more than the scratching and scraping of a
crazed, clawed animal.

'Emai *Roh*, here, replaces Emai Fohg as our resident tooth
specialist, and will be presenting his findings next Fullday.' The
director paused while Roh looked from her to the group. He
tutted in the affirmative, flattening his neck to the assembled
team, wondering; for someone amongst them knew the truth.

Someone here was paid to watch him, and to see that he got
the job done.

They moved through to breakfast – a circle of over twenty
leaning staffs arranged around a pit in the ground. Inside the pit
an old Commoner cook stooped, his sprouting, age-reddened
whiskers singed by a lifetime at the oven, busying himself with
paper parcels of food over a small fire: giant flying spiders from
the lakeshore that sizzled and squealed over the flame; fatty,
white-furred mud worms that dribbled oozing cream; singing
molluscs still caged and whimpering; weed dishes and pollen
pastes, electric yellow and blue. In the corner of the great
chamber Roh could smell the Rassus bubbling in a large
cauldron, hot and sweet. The cook glanced up as they arrived
and took their staffs, watching wryly as the scientists and
journalists mumbled their way around the circle, trying to find
the staff assigned to them. Roh found his quickly, noting with
distaste that he was between the Memorist and one of her large
assistants. He flicked his gaze around, seeing that they were still
on the far side of the circle peering at the nametags, wondering
whether he had time to switch. But by then the circle was almost
complete, and by a process of elimination the Memorist ambled
over.

The tooth specialist, yes? asked Qah, in polite Spot.

Roh tutted, placing his whiskery chin on the padded section
of the staff and locking his leg muscles straight, turning to the

21

fire as the cook threw out his first packets of boiled mollusc.

He felt the Memorist's gaze still on him, but since he couldn't see her or her spot patterns, the conversation was at a close.

'I don't suppose you'd be available for an interview later today?' Qah said carefully in Tall, a series of babbling sounds Roh couldn't pretend he hadn't heard. 'There's considerable interest in the Lake Oph dig, at least in Downway.'

He shot her the briefest of glances, allowing his irritation to show. 'I'm very busy here, I haven't time for interviews.'

She hesitated, and Roh caught a glimpse of her flank spots flickering in an exchange with Ong, on his other side. 'Of course. Well, how about a recording at Fullday, instead? After your presentation?'

His fingers paused in the unwrapping of a dish of piping hot black spider legs. *Recording.* He turned to her.

'It's just the basics,' interrupted Ong. 'What the teeth can tell us about the Oph beasts' diet, lifestyles, what have you. Our audience have some understanding of the sciences but nothing complex.'

A flash brought his head back towards Qah, and he saw that she held in her hands a tiny bulb. He glared at Ong, who cupped a dish of absorbing paper.

'For the archives,' Ong muttered, peering at it, 'hope that's all right.'

Roh's heart quickened. *No pictures.* That was one of the rules. He felt a stab of rage, discarding his half-eaten breakfast and stumbling away from the leaning staff to head for the latrines. Things were slipping and sliding already. It wasn't as simple as they'd made out.

He would need to change his plans.

'So you're from Zulzer?' asked Ong as they walked over to the cliff. Roh tutted, despairing, already set on excusing himself with a stomach ache before they could get more pictures at the site.

'We did some work over that way before the storms came in, didn't we, Qah?'

Qah arrived beside Ong, her whiskers swept back over her small ears and held in clasps. Roh could see the heat was already getting to her, and she carried her scarf in one fist. 'That's right. Droui country.'

'Oh?' he replied, hoping that would be the end of it. Those in the know had provided him with a list of academics from the region, along with falsified references and an account of a dig he'd supervised at High Morho. *You were in charge of discovering a new species, Roh*, they'd told him. *You should be very proud.*

While Qah jabbered on – in Tallspeak, for the benefit of Braldron, just behind – Roh found himself beginning to panic again. He felt his spots fluttering, his skin warming even more beneath the beating sun. The sounds of the woods, high on the clifftop, reached him like screams. He wasn't cut out for this. But they'd given him no choice. It was the only way, they'd said. *And we know you'll do it well, Roh – eschatology guild, family connections. You were meant for this job.*

He forced himself to remember those words, to focus on the memory of the fat old Commoner who'd said them to him. *You were meant for this job.*

They went deeper into the tunnels that afternoon, passing the boundary of Roh's midnight explorations and descending through the black coolness of the cliff, a fresh, water-scented waft of earth and rock prickling the coarse hairs on Roh's back. In the darkness he began to enjoy himself once more, stepping easily where others stumbled, their spots dappling the way. Tallfolk miners passed softly by, the patter of water and the roar of distant pumps soothing Roh until he began to believe in himself again. You could do anything down here, in the dark.

He let the others pass until he was at the rear of the group, the light of their spots dimming ahead, remembering the dreams of the map.

They had a person here, that much he knew. Roh was to go to the central square at Darkday and wait in the latrine. The thought of a meeting brought him out in a cold sweat once more, the darkness disorientating him. Until now he was just a fraud, visiting a place he had no right being, playing at a role he barely understood. But the game ended soon.

Some gentle, fluttering flashes up ahead, and he slowly understood that someone had turned to speak to him in the dark. It was Qah.

Are you coming, Roh?

He flickered his spots hesitantly, as if clearing his throat, and quickened his step into the cool, dripping darkness of the tunnel.

The Everywhere was a crescent of mottled, electric green and yellow continent that rose from a milky ocean so vast that nobody had ever managed to circumnavigate it. The great solitary landmass, shimmering and sweltering under eighty degree heat, was patterned with a scaled network of one thousand and eighty three triangular, walled countries belonging to the Strong and their dependent species. More than half of these states were hellish, simmering places in the grip of poverty and war and starvation, and even the vaguely functioning countries at the rim of the continent, cooled by the winds and spray of the life-rich ocean, were lands where the concept of individual freedom did not exist. From birth a Strong One could expect to be enlisted into their family guild, their careers mapped out for them, the state ensuring they were fed and watered adequately until the end of their lives: about forty-five years – or seasons – for the Strong, sixty for the Tall. Crime of any kind was punishable by excommunication to the dry continental centre, where life was short, or being hurled into the sea. Bands of hermits prowled every shoreline, always on the lookout for a way back in.

Progress in the Everywhere was slow, if not backward. The Strong had no understanding of powered flight (at over a ton in weight when fully grown, it had never seemed practical), internal combustion or even the concept of the wheel, and yet had mastered the wooden computer early on, polishing transceivers of Echowood until they shimmered and stringing their lands with conductive pipes of sea water in place of metals, which were rare and priceless and little understood.

But now the Strongfolk of the Everywhere knew one more thing, something that upset and excited them in equal measure: they were not the first advanced civilization to lay claim to their world: some other unknown master had ruled the dim and distant past when the world was young and unutterably strange.

And that master had vanished, as thoroughly as a previous tenant disappearing into the night with all their belongings – so thoroughly that the Strong had always assumed their house was new.

Five

'You'll have noticed the substance of the layer gets considerably finer the deeper we go,' Hassoh said from up ahead. Roh, whose attention was rather more drawn to the gaping skulls and boney limbs revealed glittering all around him in the weak lights of the Strongfolk spots, had not noticed. He ran his hand along the wall of the tunnel, a fine crumble of sandy rock coming away on his fingertips.

'And so we call this area the death mask,' Hassoh continued, leading them patiently into a widened section.

Roh stopped short at her sentence, looking over the heads of the Commoners in front at the opened cavity in the tunnel. A few Tallfolk squatted at work, their lanterns dangling from a line above, flashing their green and yellow eyes in the group's direction. All around them the floor of the tunnel had been opened up and roped off.

'Imprints,' Hassoh said, stooping to one side to allow them further in. 'Imprints of *faces*.'

Roh moved forward as if drawn, unable to look away. At first his eyes had trouble disentangling what was what in the gloom, none of it making any sense. And then he saw.

Images of writhing, stricken pain surrounded them, limbs and fingers outstretched, flailing. A portion of what might have been a face had pressed itself into the soft stone and howled silently in the darkness, a scream of eternity. A few that had not died instantly, that had perhaps been trapped. He felt his stomach knot, heave. Here was death in its most concentrated form, and he stood amongst it, in the middle of it, breathing in its vapours. He muttered something and excused himself, pushing his way out of the tunnel and back up towards the light.

He is kept in a wood-lined hole in the ground, like all the others, constantly under surveillance lest he attempt to burrow his way out, trying to avoid the stare of the bored Tall One assigned to watch him. Roh doesn't know how long they'll keep him here, and as he gazes around him at the claw-marked walls he wonders earnestly whether this small hole is where he'll spend the rest of his life.

A little food is dropped down by the Tall One every Twicenight, and he goes to sleep hungry each time, drowsing beneath the creature's gaze. When it rains it almost fills his hole, and he treads muddy water while the Tall One watches, impassive.

Murder. Roh was lucky not to be executed, he supposes, and after the first few days' withdrawal from that insidious drug has passed he is simply tired all the time. There are worse lives to be lived in the Everywhere. Often he wonders whether he feels less than most people. Perhaps for others this hole prison is a harsher fate.

But then, change. A day that doesn't feel the same as all the others beneath the throbbing sun. His guard disappears, replaced by a tubby old Commoner with a single blackened tooth.

'Icai Roh?'

'Yes.'

'Lucky Icai Roh.'

They take him to a place just inside the prison's borders,

a flat-topped mud town that looks out over bright green hills. Not a soul is around. Roh doesn't wonder about this; he knows who they are.

'Your family guild specialises in chemical work, yes?' the old Commoner asks him.

'It does. I do.'

'And the separation of parts?'

'I am trained in all chemical processes – I schooled at the Yolh Makery.'

'The Makery, yes. You have all the necessary skills to repay us, then.'

'Repay you? Am I getting out?'

The Commoner only gazes into his eyes. 'Why spoil it all like that? You had good prospects ahead of you.'

Roh shrugs. He doesn't owe them an explanation, though their stares say he does. Instead he catches, from the corner of his eye, a shifting shadow. It falls across the floor behind a nearby doorway. He turns his head, and it is like nothing he has ever seen.

There is something there, hidden and listening. Something... different.

Roh points numbly. 'Who's that?'

The Commoner doesn't follow his gaze. Instead he confers a little with the others by flapping his hands over his spots. When he turns back to Roh, he says simply: 'Take the job.'

Roh looks purposefully away from the shadow, seeing it shift only out of the corner of his eye.

'You will take the job, won't you?'

Roh took a basket of teeth and jaws they'd given him, setting it down inside his hut and closing the door behind him, checking the tubular waterclock on its stand. He sifted through them, carefully lifting out shards of flattened fossil and examining each in turn. Square teeth, blocks of enamel. For crunching and chomping. He couldn't stop himself imagining what it would be like to be bitten. Horrible.

The old Commoner, Vhis, had guaranteed Roh his freedom for this: freedom, and a map to better lands. Quite a promise.

Selecting the most damaged of the jawbones and setting it to one side, Roh opened his case of chemicals, taking a vial of Vorper acid in trembling fingers. He couldn't have told Vhis that he was the second worst student at the Makery, or that they'd dropped him from chemical sessions entirely and put him to work in dyes. He simply had to sit and wrack his measly brains and remember what it was they'd tried to teach him, the panic beginning to tease at the frayed edges of his mind, unravelling him thread by thread.

He checked once more to make sure the door was locked and drip-dropped the acid onto the fossil, hearing it hiss, waving away a curl of smoke. He drained some of the bubbling, steaming liquid in a crystal jar, holding it up to the light. A sediment had collected at the bottom. Roh took out a wooden spatula from his kit box and dipped it into the jar, scooping up what he could before the spatula dissolved, then tipped the rich silt onto a stone plate.

All right. Not so bad. He had something there. Was this sludge what they wanted? He peered at it, stirring it a little with the remains of the spoon, unable to know for sure.

There was a process that came next, wasn't there? Roh couldn't think, his pulse beating faster, the panic rising. Snatched memories of his classes at the Makery returned, muddled and jumbled. He remembered only one thing clearly: the Chief Maker bringing out a lump of real Gleam – so priceless that it was accompanied by two guild stewards – and using it somehow, in one of the experiments.

Roh looked at the mess he'd made on his desk. This wasn't

going to be enough for them.

He eyed the water clock, sweat dripping from his bristly chin. The level in the glass tube had sunk almost to the bottom. It was time.

He locked his door and bustled out into the square, wrapping his travel scarf around his shoulders. The sun had dropped to a smoky orange coal and settled on the line of the hills, the sky dimming to sooty blue. They would all be working through the night, and Roh didn't feel remotely tired, but the sight of it still drove some ancient mechanism – an echo of an urge to retreat back indoors.

Roh came to the latrines, the stink of which always seemed to abate slightly as the night closed in, and ducked behind the wall to the pits. There was nobody there, and he leaned, restless, in the mud, relieving himself while he wondered who it was going to be.

Their contact had apparently been here for some time, preparing the groundwork. Had they seen him already? Sniffed him out? Roh had no idea how subtle he had really been. The Organisation – the Commoners who'd rescued him from a lifetime in a hole in the ground – had said the contact would be ready. But whoever it was, they were late.

Footsteps outside at last, and Roh stiffened, watching the wall. He could tell at once that the soft pitter-patter belonged to a Tall One, and knew before the person revealed themselves who it would be.

Unph Braldron rounded the corner cautiously, eyeing him.

'Hmm,' he mumbled at last, leaning back against the wall so that he had a vantage of anyone crossing the square.

'Not who you were expecting?' asked Roh, eyeing the black, hair-like tufts that decorated Braldron's stick-thin limbs.

'Had my suspicions,' he replied, his beak folding out into a chuckle.

'Do you think anyone else suspects?' Roh asked earnestly,

leaning forward and pronouncing the odd noises as carefully as he could.

Braldron appeared to think. 'No. Hassoh's too wrapped up in it all. The others don't see yet what could be stolen from here – they haven't realised the extent of the prize.' He shot Roh a glance. 'We have to get a move on. Have you extracted Gleam yet? Do you have any?'

Roh looked away, into the odd, oily shimmer of the slurry pit. It was growing so dark that he could only see the glint and flutter of the lambent Suckleflies as they enjoyed their feast. 'That box you gave me – I did everything I could, but...'

'But?' He sensed the Tall One staring at him.

'I don't think it works the way your – our – employers think it does.'

'It has to,' Braldron said sharply. 'They said it would. You were chosen precisely because you said you could do it.'

'I made no promises – I had to send for advice, to the Eschatology guild at Buree,' Roh whispered. 'They never replied.'

'*Advice?*' Braldron's breathing was suddenly loud.

'I didn't know -'

'You sent for advice?' the Tall One snapped. 'You're out. You're *done*. That wasn't –'

'Let me finish,' Roh said, more forcibly. 'I didn't tell them what I wanted to know all this for. And I think it can be done, I just need some time. And more equipment.'

'Equipment? What equipment? We only have a few days.'

'I need some Gleam to start with, in order to extract more, I think.'

Braldron studied him, a lanky shadow in the dimness, his chest rising and falling. 'You're joking. Playing me for a fool.'

'It's a process we call, um, Spark-Mirroring,' Roh growled, making up the name on the spot. 'It's the only way to do it, I think.' He watched the glittering flies. 'Either that, or we just –'

he shrugged a spot shrug, the coloured pores flaring on only one side of his body – 'ship them out on the barges, crumbled to powder, and they can work out how to do it themselves.'

Braldron fell silent for a long time. At last he stood, a full hand above Roh, a tapering, teetering shadow with long, gruesome fingers. 'Let me know what you need, *exactly*, and we shall see what can be done.' He reached out a finger and tapped Roh on the belly. 'And the names of those you sent to for advice. They can't talk, you know that. You've cursed them.'

'But I told you, they never replied –'

'Tough.' And with that, Braldron was gone.

Roh stumbled back into the square a while after, his breathing only just coming under control. He still felt nauseous, even after vomiting.

He looked to the forest, dark against the blizzard of newly risen stars, wondering if he could run. He would become one of those hermits he read about, a foot soldier in the tattered army that clogged the shores and caves. His life would be short, but longer than any left to him if he stayed.

Unless he could do as they asked. He thought again of that mind-bending shadow he'd seen in the prison doorway. Something belonging to a creature the likes of which he'd never seen. Something that could not exist here, on this world.

His eyes moved to the stars, studying their flow. Most of the Everywhere thought they were spirits, hanging glowing overhead. They each had names and stories, and their colours and scintillations were still interpreted by Strong prophets into strange and ridiculous gobbledygook, spot-colour whispers from the night sky. To a creature like Roh, who spoke in such ways, the stars did seem to talk – a mutter of muted colour, like an echo. But it said nothing he could comprehend, and as a member of a scientific guild he knew better what they were: distant relatives of his own sun, with worlds that fed from their light.

That shadow had come from above.

Roh went back to his hut, peeking for a long time through the window at the moonless night, wondering if it was too late. After a time he turned back to his box of teeth, performing more experiments that steamed and sizzled, feeling no closer to the solution than before.

The priceless Gleam and Glitter locked in these fossils had been known about for some time, the Underworld having concealed the first findings of other beasts like these from the population. For some unknown reason, the Lake Oph beasts contained within their bones levels of minerals that simply did not exist in the world, as if they had eaten it all in the great long ago.

What Gleam Strongfolk possessed had always come from trace veins and falling stars, the meteors chiselled into staves for the rulers of old, stronger and sharper than the Echowood swords everyone else used; it had given the ancient kings their power, and it was needed now, needed for something Roh had no understanding of, something beyond his function to know.

There was a thump outside: someone stomping their foot up and down to make their presence known. Roh turned, startled, and peered through the little hatch in the door.

It was Qah, waiting with a drink in one hand and her blasted flash equipment in the other. Roh backed softly away from the door, gathering up his things as silently as he could until his bag was swiftly packed and slung around his neck, and climbed out of the far window, heading for the black line of woods.

Six

He couldn't tell if anyone was following in the dark. As he left the borders of the dig site the sounds of the Slaughterwoods grew so loud that they drowned any footsteps behind him. Panicking, Roh dithered, blindly swivelling his head this way and that. He had no choice now. He turned back in the direction of the woods, following the soft glow of the lakeshore, the mud squeezing between his toes.

He didn't dare light his lantern, in case Braldron or the others saw it from the camp. The forest reared blackly ahead, a blaze of stars lighting the glossy mud. Roh had seen a map of the region. He knew he was moving along the curve of the lake to the narrow stretch of woods that opened out into fields and farmland, but the distances were a mystery. What he thought of as a small ridge of woodland could be a day or more across. He hadn't packed food, or water, just his useless wooden computer, his tools and the basket of fossil jaws, all weighing heavily in the bag around his neck.

As the darkness of the woods drew closer, Roh stumbled to a standstill, his legs caked in shining mud, looking back the way he'd come. Across the shore the camp's lights twinkled, workers and miners and excavators and scientists still going about their jobs. Roh felt a certain deathly, exhausted freedom from it all.

He was going his own way now.

He looked back to the darkness, loud with calls and mutters and screams, aware that it was madness to enter before dawn. But Braldron could be anywhere. Roh adjusted the chafing strap of his bag a little and hurried on.

He came to the grasses and weeds, the sting of thorns and bites cutting into his ankles. Roh hobbled on one leg, blindly searching in his pack until he found the second set of wooden boots crumpled at the bottom, and pulled them on, one muddy foot after the other, almost falling. He wrapped his scarf around his neck, jamming his wooden hat onto his head, finally taking out the paddle weapon he'd kept stored in a hidden pouch. He turned it in his hands, aware that he could make out the long, flat shape of the thing, and when he looked up again the stars in the east had begun to fade, some suggestion of light paling the sky. He looked towards the woods.

Already they shimmered, a riot of colours unfurling with the first light, each tone and hue competing for a mate. Roh knew back home what was dangerous in the woods; here he had no clue. He would need to tread lightly, stay awake for as long as it took. He went in.

At once the light dimmed almost to nothing, a murk of shadows and muted colour, sighing and muttering around him. The night creatures that screamed and cried were all bedding down now, their replacements just waking up, and a rare silence enveloped the woods. Roh could hear his own grunting progress, shoving and hacking at tendrils and membranes and stems, their forms recoiling from his approach. Something alighted on his shoulder and stung him, and he swept it wildly away, heart thumping. In his other hand he held his paddle, the pouch of stone ammunition dangling from it, though he couldn't see more than a few steps ahead in the gloom.

These woods, Roh knew, had never been cleared. For as

long as the Strong and the Tall had existed they had avoided the lush hills, building their towns in the expanses of dry desert in between, channelling canals and tributaries to serve their needs. But in the world there lived other clever things, that spoke and built and hunted with tools, and some made the Slaughterwoods their home. He imagined it had occurred to many on the run that they could find refuge in the woods, and wondered how long any of them lasted.

The world around him lightened, the colours intensifying from unfurling petals and leaves, blazing crimson and cobalt and bright shimmering green. The trunks, spotted yellow, were actually segmented groupings of spider-like legs, and at the vibrations of Roh's advance they shuffled and twitched. He gave them a wide berth, weapon clutched tight, scanning the canopies and watching for holes amongst the undergrowth, moving so slowly that he could imagine Braldron catching up with him at any moment. Great hand-sized insects fluttered through the gaps in the branches, settling on the drooling teeth of honey-coated mouths, to be snapped up. Furred, patterned serpents hung from the canopies like coloured ribbons, their jaws agape, eyes closed. Tree molluscs scampered and danced, flashing dazzling displays from their electrified, branching shells.

Roh was wrapped in the scents of it all, a cloud of competing pheromones thrown together, his weak nose overwhelmed by it all. Tears stung his eyes, sneezes paralysed him. He shuffled faster, blundering, a thousand drooping tongues and feelers slithering wetly across his body as he pushed his way through. He felt the blood from a bite running warmly down his back, and the pulsing suckle of a hanging parasite. Something swarmed in his ear, trying to drill its way in, and another climbed clumsily up his nose. He stopped, slapping himself and crying out, the life around him pausing to watch. Eyes that glowed and pulsed, plant nostrils quivering as they inhaled his stink, a swarming cloud of spiders, drifting beneath silken parachutes, their furred legs outstretched. A creeping, twig-like thing came jerking out behind a branch, inspecting him with coiling eyestalks before moving on.

The biting resumed, nibbling, tasting, lapping. A dozen tiny feet scampered across his skin. Roh was being digested alive already, like food in the gut – he had wandered into an ecosystem that would eat him slowly from the outside in, until his bones were dissolved and his minerals - so cheap and common in comparison to the stuff he'd been sent here to extract - returned to the world. He caught a hint of movement out of the corner of his eye: a flicker of something larger than anything he'd yet seen, and froze, his parasites forgotten.

It peered at him from the depths, and he peered back.

A child? he flashed in Spotspeak.

Its face was dark and wide-eyed, the spitting image of a Strong person in their first year, and yet it felt even more familiar. It was like looking into a distorted mirror, as if Roh had encountered a younger brother or sister, lost out here in the wilderness. He stepped forward, numb, trying to see it better. It even wore a broad-brimmed wooden hat, like him.

And then he saw, hidden in the undergrowth, a neck and body, pale and then livid, venereal pink, extending from a weed-shrouded cavern in the ground. Roh's mind tried to adjust to what he saw, to separate the child's wide-eyes from that gruesome column of flesh, and yet still he moved forward, towards its whimpering, snivelling face. The neck pulsed, expectant, and he tensed his fingers on the paddle. The whimpering ceased.

It shot forward, unravelling across the forest at him, and he thwacked a sharpened pebble into the sickly tube of lunging body, spraying blood across the trees. The thing bucked and writhed and flew backwards, the child's face vanishing as it angled its mirrored, concave face, the illusion shattering. Roh screamed and it screamed back, sucking back into its burrow and disappearing.

He stood where he was, the waft of descending stink and blood shrouding him, then bolted deeper into the woods.

Roh came out into direct sunlight a full day later, staggering, wheezing. The tall flowered grasses peered at him and shrunk into their hard carapaces, sucking down to expose the land beyond.

He stared, almost blind in one eye from the swelling of a bite, his skin livid and raw, the backs of his legs smeared with shit and urine, gasping at the thinner, fresher air.

Across the plain, herds of mammalian Hiiorhies moved ponderously at the borders of a lake, hoovering the meadow grasses with their four slobbering mouths. It was another in the Ophiphi cluster, perhaps Opo, or Uhm. Which meant he hadn't come far at all. The Hiiorhies' songs, issuing from great nostrils on their backs, travelled like distant, rolling thunder, grumbling across the plain, and Roh locked his legs to squat as the wind soothed his ruined skin. He watched a Berl, a hairy, long-horned predator the size and weight of a Strong One dwelling, lying and panting listlessly within sight of the herd.

Roh turned his attention to the ridge he stood upon, gazing past some scrawny tufts of Flusswood to what looked like a signpost. He ambled over, reading the spots of paint.

NIHNLO THE TOWN

It lay in the dip of the hills, the scrub and stubble cleared for almost a mile in all directions beyond the ring of a deep, dry moat. Echowood and colourstone drawbridges led across the moat to a wooden township of two-storey dwellings, their towers looking out over the Slaughterwoods.

Roh came down the ridge, feeling watched. He had a large wooden guild medallion around his neck, and clutched it to him.

It was all that stood between him and destitution, for the bearer of this medallion was entitled to food and lodging wherever they went – provided it was in date, of course. Luckily for Roh he'd had his stamped not long ago, but in less than a slow year it would be unusable, and he would have to think of some other way.

He arrived at the southerly drawbridge, gazing down into the pit below. Bones littered the shadows, gaping skulls and teeth interspersed with groves of whispering carrion flowers, rubbish, offal, pieces of busted equipment. He caught movement, noticing some scavengers wandering down there with great sacks on their backs, sorting. Roh pulled the medallion from the folds of his scarf, holding it up for a dark figure seated on the far side of the moat. Its eyes glittered, and he realised it was one of the Still. *Come*, he thought it had said. The colour alphabet they expressed through their eyes was similar to a Strong One's spotspeak, and after a moment's thought he replied with what he hoped was a *thank you*, venturing out across the wobbly drawbridge.

The figure at the far end was indeed what he imagined it to be, sitting stooped upon a wooden stool. Its blue-black skin looked burnished by sunlight, years spent sitting in this place, waiting to greet the few visitors to the town.

They were an odd sort, of another, separate family line from the Strong and Tall; probably risen from the sea, like the Strong, in the great long ago. The Still One's small, flat face looked out from its midriff, long nostrils coiling beneath its eyes and dropping to a mouth that was little more than a drooling slit of skin.

Roh met its large watery eyes and a feast of colour rose inside them, blending and separating, forming a whisper of unspoken words that his conditioned brain instinctively understood.

From?

39

Zulzer, Roh answered back in Spotspeak. *I need lodging, for a day or two.*

The creature's eyes cleared, draining to bulbous amber bubbles, the pupils engorging, before a flood of colour rose once more from a scattering of faint wells inside the iris. Roh found himself reading the spreading pools of pink and cream and blue in the wrong order, and forced himself to concentrate.

Go to the Staffhouse, ask for Yu.
She will give you what you need.

Roh tutted his thanks, finding the eyes slightly unsettling, and passed through the simple wooden gate to follow the line of canal. Rosy colourstone buildings roofed with Echowood slabs rose on either side, their occupants slumbering in what was now the Twicenight, though Roh's scrambled brains insisted it was a sun-drenched late afternoon. He spied barges on the canal further up, reading the painted colours along their sides. *Nihnlo fishery guild.* A state building further along announced itself with a bright pattern of dots across its eaves: *Nihnlo Town Register,* and Roh stepped into the shade of the street, watchful. A barge loaded with Thrisselwood moved sluggishly past, poled by Tallfolk at the prow and stern, and Roh watched until it was out of sight, headed for the mill he'd spotted further along. A single, finely spun cloud drifted overhead.

Roh followed a dirty tributary of the central canal and found Yu's lodging house, secreted in the shadows of an alley.

A Strongfolk child was sitting in the sun at the end of the lane, and Roh slowed, remembering the ordeal in the forest. Mind Messers were common enough in woodlands, but not in civilization.

It sat still, watchful. Strongfolk did not play like the Tall Ones did, either in youth or adulthood. Their children sat still as ornaments, observing, drinking in the world around them, not socialising until around their tenth year, when their Spotspeak began to develop. Roh faintly remembered his childhood as a period of intense quiet and contemplation, a silent, introspective life in which, after a short spell of weaning and instruction, he spoke to nobody. He thought little of his biological parents, who had left him at the guild without attachment, and even less of his own progeny somewhere out in the world. To the constant bewilderment of the Tall, the Strong needed little entertainment besides the satisfaction of their jobs and the pleasures of food and sleep, taking simple delight in the basics of life.

He passed the child warily – taking one last look to make sure it *was* a child – its silent stare following him all the way to the door.

Inside the air was cool, the entrance in shadow. He waited a while by the door to see who would come, flickering a dim hello to the proprietor when she did. He had woken her, but was so tired himself that he couldn't think of how to apologise, so he kept silent. She was Strong, like him, and clothed in feather-soled slippers and scarf. After a wordless glance at his medallion, her eyes lingering on the date stamp, she went behind a counter and heaved out a sleeping staff, passing it to Roh. He inspected the stained padding, not daring to ask for another, and followed her along a snaking hallway into the darkness of the slumbering house.

The cook had woken up, too, and waited for them with a sour expression on his wrinkled face, stoking a small fire. Roh flashed gratitude without getting much of a reply, and locked his legs to lean against the staff, watching the Commoner's hands as they assembled some parcels of canal weed and treeleapers, then heated them over the fire.

He ate as quickly as he could, stuffing everything into his mouth as soon as it was given to him and signalling his thanks brightly, then took up his staff and waddled into the shadows of the adjoining chamber, feeling his way to an unoccupied, windowless cell. He had thought of staying up a while to keep a

Tom Toner

lookout, but the street outside was silent, the snorts and grumbles of the other guests soothing, and before his brain knew what was happening he was fast asleep.

Seven

He woke late, blinking at the faint light drifting into his cell, the commotion of breakfast and washing filtering from the next rooms. Someone had used seeing mixture in the night; Roh could smell it – a cloying stench that awoke long buried urges in him. The flower paste, rubbed onto the skin and left to dry, was too strong for the Tall, but popular amongst Strongfolk down on their luck. Roh had known it well.

When he peeked his head out of his space, the sleeping chamber was empty, a mess of strewn sleeping staffs and rubbish, full pots of piss sitting waiting to be collected. Roh used his quickly, squatting down and locking his legs, trying to ignore the dispersing stink of the seeing mixture and remembering bit by bit why he was there.

His pulse quickened. The Twicenight was long over: they would know by now that he had gone.

He decided to forego breakfast and washing, and left by the front door without a word to anyone. The child was nowhere to be seen, the town now bathed in a blush of rosy evening sunlight that brought out the electric greens and pinks and yellows of the hills beyond.

He had a thought and ducked his head back inside the boarding house, working his way through the milling workers and fisherfolk as they brushed themselves down until he found the proprietor again. She was tipping out the bowls.

Excuse me.

She did not look at him. *You are excused.*

Roh pointed to the door, and the implication of the canal beyond. *Is there a barge leaving any time soon?*

She looked him over quickly, a dribble of urine slopping on her feet from one of the bowls. *There was one supposed to be in last Twicenight, but it was late. Might be there now.*

He flashed a quick thanks and stumbled out again, her eyes following him, his bellies rumbling as the waft of breakfast coiled from the surrounding buildings, heart beating harder at the prospect of a quick getaway. His medallion would take him anywhere in the world, for as long as it lasted. He did the maths in his head as he entered the main causeway, knowing it was a small year to the middle of the world from here, his spirits falling. He wouldn't get as far as he'd like before the medallion was useless, and the punishment for forging date stamps was instant death.

But a moment later he forgot his despair: filling the canal further down was a vast rectangle of flat raft, its deck piled high with cargo, a teetering signal tower rising from one end. Roh looked right and left at the small crowd come to survey the novelty of the raft, their shadows long, and made his way quickly to the stone cargo dock.

A fanning queue had already formed, and he wished again that he'd woken earlier. Most were mill workers headed for their jobs, but Roh glimpsed a few travelers with heavy packs – specialists heading up-way to unknown work, or returning from long stints somewhere behind – waiting to see if there would be space. Roh's medallion was no better than any other, and he would have to wait his turn with the workers, so he locked his muscles once more and prepared to wait out the evening as they reloaded the raft. As he waited he looked up the street to the

44

state building, its spotwork emblem almost glowing in the sinking sun, and saw a figure standing there, watching the crowd. Roh fancied he met the distant figure's eyes, and when he did it moved slowly and hesitantly back inside.

He felt his blood warm. They'd sent word ahead. The crowd was watched.

Roh could think of nothing for it but to try to move closer towards the bank, threading his way amongst the jostling crowd. He got a few meters before the first flickers of protest went up, and when he reached the bank he pulled out his medallion for the shipmaster to see.

What's the rush? the Commoner asked, peering down at him with one milky eye, his snaggle-tooth clamped around a spot brush.

Order business, he said, shaking the medallion; the penalty for misuse, another death. He was accumulating them; why stop now? *From Emai Phig Hassoh, director of the Oph works.*

The Commoner took the brush out of his mouth and glanced at his wooden ledger. *Hassoh. Had a few of hers come through. All right, where do you need to go?*

Roh hesitated. *Ottel?*

The Commoner flashed a spot shrug and helped Roh aboard, to the consternation of everyone he'd shoved past. Roh glanced at them without a word and moved to the far side of the raft, where the air was cooler and cleaner, hoping the most vocal of them wouldn't be allowed on. This was going to be a long journey.

Slowly the raft filled up, its lower decks stuffed with as many bodies as it could carry, the cargo level sinking almost to the waterline. Roh remained on deck but kept his head down, looking at his feet, waiting to be gone. By sundown they were stocked and ready to leave, the queue of remaining hopefuls dispersing, lights kindling in the town as it slipped slowly away into the dark. Roh raised his head at last, the breeze welcome as he took off his hat, listening to forested banks as they slid by. Strongfolk and Commoners and Moy-people lumbered up and down the decks, watching the night go by, almost silent. Those on their way to the mill and fishery were commuting to work, and the enjoyment of the journey was lost on them. To Roh it was like the beginning of the holidays – a lifetime's holiday that would only end with his death.

He watched the night shine of eyes in the woods and experienced a shudder of excitement that soon cooled to fear. Ottel was just the first place he'd thought of. He would have to get to the coast, he supposed, where all the rest of the rubbish ended up, somewhere he couldn't be found. Would they stop looking? Probably. To be exiled was to be lost, as good as dead.

There didn't seem to be any food aboard, besides what the workers brought with them, and so Roh went up to the tower to wait out his hunger. He saw the lights of the mill as soon as he was up top, and stopped to watch the installation as it approached. A sprawling complex of wooden, smoking towers rose from the cleared land, their peaks lost in shadow. The canal widened as more tributaries joined it, their waters glittering with light, and the bargefolk began their poling to the bank. Roh turned on his platform to survey the workers making ready to leave, the tops of their heads passing by below him.

There, lit only by irregularly spaced lanterns, a Tall One strolled alongside. He examined the workers as they shuffled off, eyes moving amongst their shadowed faces, before turning back to the barge.

Roh met his gaze. Braldron.

They arrived back at camp before Twicenight, following a canal that ran parallel with the lake system as sunrise coloured the east. The herds of Hiiorhies Roh had seen from the ridge must have moved on, and the plains had looked vast and empty from his position on Braldron's small wooden boat.

Hassoh wasn't there to meet them, though Roh glimpsed her at the entrance to the operations cone as he trudged back to his hut, Braldron close at his heels. The irritation caused by his desertion was palpable, and it seemed, from the glances of the workers, that Braldron had not been spared, either. He'd concocted some story to explain their jaunt to Nihnlo town, but it was clear the camp couldn't spare him.

They came to the hut and went inside together. A pile of spot sheets and more baskets of fossils had been deposited at the entrance, and Roh shoved it all inside with his foot. Braldron said nothing until he'd closed the door behind them.

'You have your work now. Get on with it.'

Roh surveyed the baskets of fossils.

'That was your one strike, Roh,' Braldron continued, flopping into a Tall chair he'd obviously brought in here during Roh's absence. 'There's no second.'

Roh began sorting through his equipment and laying it out on the table. 'I told you, I'll try.'

Braldron remained sitting. 'I'm going to watch for a while, see how you do it.'

And so Roh began his useless experiments once more, hating the stare of the thing that watched him from the chair, utterly dejected to find himself back here once more, working on something that could not be done. But he tried new things nonetheless, crunching the stone tablets to powder and immersing them in water, before running a charge through the mixture using the near-priceless pieces of Gleam Braldron had brought him, dull things that looked as if they'd been handled by hundreds of grubby, greedy fingers. Near the bottom of the fossil pile, amongst the flattened jaw bones of a dozen or more individuals, lay a small, indented impression, like a perfectly square leaf engraved with a filigree of interconnected channels so thin and delicate that the pattern looked almost natural. Roh inspected it for a moment, turning it in his clumsy fingers, before putting it back. Braldron watched with vague interest until his shadow yawned, and he stood up.

'I'll let you work in peace now. But you *must* work.' The shadow hesitated, considering the back of Roh's head. 'Are we agreed?'

Roh tutted his assent, busying himself, hearing the Tall One pause for some time outside his door to listen. At length the presence sighed and slunk away, muttering something under his breath.

The day grew hotter as the last of the stragglers went to their beds. Roh had laid his tools down some time ago, and was staring vacantly out of the window, thinking. Everything he'd tried had failed, and yet he was oddly calm. There was only one thing for it, really.

Roh opened his door a crack and peered out into the sunny landscape. The heat shimmered like sweat rising from the ground, the jungle baked. Smog cast a faded curtain across the spires of the central cone, orange and dusty. Roh stepped out and locked his door, walking into the shimmer.

At the shore of the lake he plunged his toes into cool mud, sloshing into the water and bobbing up to his chin. His bones were light enough – and the lake so salty – that he needn't tread water and simply hung in the murk, thick arms outspread. He sunk his head beneath the water, blowing out a muffled stream of bubbles, the cool shade absorbing him entirely, and felt at last free of the world. He could drown himself here and now, if only he could sink.

No, it would have to be done. Braldron was all that stood in the way. Roh's submerged mind balked at the thought, holding closed a door that swung easily open. But the coldness of the lake had numbed him, and as he rose back into sunlight he remembered it all.

The urges happened only every four years or so: a cycle in which the female Strong came into oestrus, the males itched and ached and swelled down below, a gland in their abdomens developing over a month or so into a stiffened lump of oozing flesh. Both males and females grew silly with hormones, acting drunk and foolish, the sobriety of Strongfolk society cast aside. Infrastructure ground to a standstill, jobs were forgotten and barges ceased to run as the population decorated their bodies and left their homes. Males were suddenly no longer able to talk to each other and only grunted or growled, prowling the land like a drunk craving food.

Roh remembered his mating dimly, clouded as it had been by a fog of Rassus spirit and seeing mixture, the sense of arousal as abstract to him now as a half-forgotten dream. All he recalled was that, in the throes of his second Wanting, he had killed. And for that he had spent almost three slow years imprisoned in a hole in the ground.

It wasn't uncommon. Prisons in the Everywhere were filled with crimes of passion, often exacerbated by the use of seeing mixture, or Juice. The punishment for *any* misdemeanour – no matter how small – was a minimum of lifelong incarceration in a hole in the ground or a plunge into the sea, a maximum of slow, tortuous death for the perpetrator and indefinite hereditary servitude to one's old guild. It was different for the Tallfolk, who, being a different people long unified by ancient agreement, operated under their own branch of the laws. They looked upon the Strong with pitying disdain, Roh was sure – free folk living side by side with their backwards neighbours, a lively people who appreciated entertainments of fiction and dance, neither of which the Strong, with their vastly different minds, could fathom.

Roh couldn't even remember the person he'd killed, or much of the act itself, and the memory – pored over so often during his time in the hole – was now so well-thumbed that he doubted its integrity altogether, like a sentence repeated until it was no longer the same. Someone, some belligerent Strong male, had got in his way. He recalled a flare of spots, a snarl and tussle, the mauling of tiny sharp teeth and his own rage and fury. And then the scent of a female and the hunger of the chase, the fight forgotten until they'd forced him to remember. For he had been seen, and there was no getting out of it. Trials did not exist, just the word of the crowd, and as such he had been sent to his fate without even learning the name of his victim, or who had struck the first blow.

And now he would do it all over again.

Roh looked across the water to the camp, wondering how. His gaze moved along to the distant, turreted cone, its colourstone slopes faded by the sun.

He turned himself around in the water until he could see the far shore, where a distant harbour lay drifting in the shimmer.

Perhaps there was another way.

A flicker of colour startled his floating reverie. It was Qah, wading out towards him.

I thought we weren't supposed to swim in the lake.

He watched her sinking up to her wrinkled wattle of neck, then gaze around her at the surface of the water. *Is it safe? I heard there were Stranglerfish.*

Roh had no idea; the thought hadn't even occurred to him. He looked between the dim suggestion of his outstretched legs and shrugged.

Tang doesn't think our trip's been much of a success, Qah said. Now they had stopped splashing Roh could see some smaller fish and water ninnies flitting in the weak light beneath his toes.

We're being called back after the presentations, she said. *There's not much interest in the dig.*

Roh looked at her a while as he lay floating, suspecting that might change soon enough.

'Braldron.'

'Huh?' a clatter of beak in the dimness.

Roh crept in, his eyes taking their time to adjust to the dark. 'Braldron. I know what we need to do.'

The stick-thin shadow did not stir. 'Did you manage it? Is it working?'

Roh dropped his head in the darkness. 'I think, to get any worthwhile amounts of Gleam, you need a lot of the fossils, powdered up.'

'So you've failed?'

'I'm saying I know another way.'

The shadow leant and kindled its lamp, and suddenly Braldron was watching him from the corner.

Roh squatted on his haunches. 'There's going to be a presentation, in the operations building. They'll have a lot of the specimens in there. Afterwards, when everyone's asleep, we stoke up the heaters and melt it all down. I looked at the tracks they laid, it's all still in place. We can take everything out of here in one go, out across the lake.'

Braldron fell silent for some time, his spindly fingers laced, the lantern roaring softly at his side.

Eight

And so he found himself before the assembled diggers, preparators, technicians and staff. Even the cook had ambled into the wings to watch, his hands black with Gurri flour. Roh had already leaned, fidgeting, through a presentation on the creatures by one of the diggers, who had explained something only half intelligible about the sounds the Oph beasts could have made as well as the capacity of their skulls, which might or might not have contained well-developed brains, or some other organ the Strong could not envisage – perhaps a bladder, if they were indeed aquatic. Roh had looked at the diagram of a round, open skull – quite different from a Strong person's soft, flattened little pouch at the base of their necks – but his eyes kept wandering to the three large ceramic furnaces stationed at each corner of the central chamber, then in the direction of the woodpile out back.

It would soon be his turn, and he lumbered from the safety of his leaning staff and into their field of view, fluttering his spots in diffident recognition of the assembled group while Thiim, who was first, prepared his models. Braldron watched from the back, his mind also clearly far away as he considered the fine collection of fossils stored upstairs, ready for transportation, and Roh wondered just what would happen if he exposed the whole thing now, to all the assembled Eschatologists. Braldron would deny it, denounce him as a fantasist. But Roh's eyes strayed to Hassoh, knowing she suspected something was up. *She* would believe.

'Emai Icai Roh', she said to Roh in Tallspeak, singling him out. 'Of Zulzer, renowned discoverer of the Hyaphile hoard and decorated expert on dentition.' He locked eyes with her, understanding faintly from the tone of her Tallspeak that she was still furious with him for his absence. She directed her attention back to the assembly while she spoke. 'You have been analysing the teeth and jaws and suchlike, and will have much to tell us after Emai Hem Thiim is done, yes?'

He smiled a weak, anxious spot smile as the Memorist Ong turned his refilled equipment on the group once more, flashing and flickering as it recorded moving images. Qah herself was not present, ill apparently and confined to her hut. Roh supposed that when she awoke, he'd be gone.

'Dwellings,' Thiim began, stepping behind his great model of honeycombed clay and taking up a thin, Thrisselwood pole so that he could point at all the tiny details he'd worked so hard on.

While Thiim spoke, Roh watched the local Luphri catcher, Gioh, as he stalked down the winding stair behind the assembled crowd. Usually his pots were full of the squealing, squirming things, but today they seemed to be empty.

The colour surge of applause brought him back to reality, the glow of spots dazzling the chamber, and Thiim stepped down.

Roh tried not to meet Hassoh's eye as he opened up the spotsheets he'd prepared that morning, rooting through the baskets of teeth and deciding at last to hand them out. The tiny chunk of imprinted, linear structure lurked at the bottom of his scraps and bones, scratched from lying beneath a pile of other slabs. Roh barely looked at the thing as he took it out and stuffed it in one of the pouches dangling from his scarf – he did not know what it was, and it couldn't help him now. For the hundredth time Roh wished he'd paid more attention during the medical stages of his training, when they'd looked at old leathery corpses gifted to the guild, pulling them apart for the students; Roh had always found some excuse to look away, dipping his finger into the spot paint and stippling aimless notes.

He opened his mouth to speak, his mind going perfectly blank. Some of the assembly were already muttering to themselves, flickers of Spotspeak and grunts, and Roh broke into a sweat, heart pounding harder until he became aware of the sound of something from outside. A pause, heavy with silence.

A cry erupted from outside. Roh closed his mouth as a few Tallfolk at the front headed to the entrance. It had sounded like Tang.

Hassoh scowled, holding up a hand to Roh and lumbering to the doorway, the Tallfolk already congregating behind her.

Roh and Braldron passed one another briefly by the furnace while the last of the workforce rushed out into the late sunlight to see what all the commotion was about. Roh fingered the tiny piece of stone in his scarf pocket, their eyes meeting, before joining the others outside.

He gazed across the flat ground towards the dwellings, where people were already crowding around. It was not Tang's cone they went to, but Qah's.

Roh followed them, picking up speed.

'Something – a creature...' Tang was muttering as Roh approached the cone.

Roh pushed his way through the crowd, smelling something thick in the interior air, and peered over Tang's shoulder.

Pieces of Qah lay everywhere, seemingly flung, as if she'd been dropped into a rotating fan. He recognised her only by the grey-white tone of her shredded skin. Roh stared. He'd never seen so much blood before; it coated every object in the hut with a thin varnish. What was clear was that the bulk of her was gone – her head and torso, all taken away. Roh turned instinctively, as if the culprit might be right behind him, and met the eyes of the arriving Tallfolk. He stumbled out, looking right and left, passing more arriving people drawn to the hut by Tang's screams. A group of hunters who made their camp at the edge of the wood came sprinting down the slope, their paddle weapons ready, calling for people to get inside. Roh stumbled and realised he'd trodden in a blood-speckled footprint, deep and clawed. He went to the woodpile, mind blank with shock, and took what he needed for the furnaces, making his way back towards the operations cone.

Inside the heat was already palpable, the furnaces ablaze with stacked kindling. Braldron had lit them early, perhaps anticipating a curfew. Roh dropped his armfuls of wood and went between each of the great ceramic pots, stuffing logs and branches inside them and scalding his fingers as he closed each door. There was no sign of Braldron, besides a soft, whimpering whine drifting down from the floor above. Roh stopped to listen. Someone was up there, creaking the wooden floorboards. He stumbled upstairs, still numb with visions of the mutilated Qah.

The first thing he saw was Braldron across the room, backed between two great stacks of Lake Oph fossils, paralysed with fear. In the centre of the room lay the remains of the cook, similarly consumed from the inside out, a spray of blood decorating the floor.

Roh had come upon it from behind; an iridescent, scaled apparition almost the length of the upper floor, huffing wheezing breaths as it scented the air. Its tail wagged silkily as it advanced on Braldron, vestigial wings flapping with excitement, and Roh recognized it only from pictures: a Leth, from the lake. It must have followed the scent of dinner.

Roh still had a shard of fossil in his hand – the imprint of the strange square leaf – and clasped its hard edge between his fingers, ready to strike. The thing, still unaware of Roh's presence behind it, slunk a step closer to Braldron, whose whimpering grew shrill.

'Do something!' Braldron shrieked at Roh. The Leth hesitated, began to turn in Roh's direction. Roh could hear its breathing quickening, and knew there was nothing to be done.

He backed away, carefully negotiating the stair without making a sound. The furnaces were roaring, the walls already beginning to sag inwards. He waited another moment, cringing at Braldron's high-pitched, lunatic scream, then stole outside, sealing the doorway shut behind him.

Roh stepped back, watching the cone's peaked spires bubble and deflate. A hint of sound drifted to him, cut suddenly short.

'I've trapped the thing inside!' Roh cried to the nearest Tallfolk, who had come to watch the cone melt. They barely gave him a second glance as he set out in the direction of the harbour.

Nine

The Strong weren't supposed to have nightmares; those were the preserve of the Tallfolk, who often woke screaming in the nights. But now Roh knew them too. The thing, the creature with the impossible shadow, scuttled after him in his dreams, creeping closer, never seen.

Roh woke on the multicoloured sand of the shore and rubbed his overgrown whiskers. He'd hidden himself for the Twicenight in a crag of weed-caked rocks, and the tide had risen almost to his knees, the salt stinging. He blinked and reached into the water, retrieving the polished ammunition he'd been sharpening as he fell asleep.

It was time to move on, always as soon as he woke, ever since that... *rune*, whatever you called it, the drawing, had appeared one day beside his temporary camp. He'd examined it only for as long as he needed to see that it wasn't spot writing or Tall words, then gathered up his belongings and left at a shambling run, keeping up the pace until he thought his heart would burst.

It felt like half a lifetime, tramping the never-ending northern shore, a sack of his few possessions hung always around his neck, the unending chafe of salt and sand peeling his skin into thick pink ropes that scabbed black in the sun. In one fist he held a spear of Echowood, tipped with the hard shard of fossil he'd taken with him, its curious synthetic leaf imprint decorating the blade, and in the other his paddle weapon, the clinking hide pouch of ammunition tied around his waist.

Roh never found out what that shadow had wanted – surely not anything as basic as Gleam. Braldron had hinted one night that he had an idea, that he was searching for something else amongst the graves, but that was close to the end, and Roh never discovered what the Tall One was after. The stars were a mystery to the peoples of the Everywhere, the name for their world coined in antiquity – between the two distinct epochs which had seen a cohesive, centrally ruled world rise, fall then rise once more – and made more ironic every time they peered further into the night sky. The Strong knew of five planets, named after their last five kings, and had called the stars by names Roh had mostly forgotten, but which he watched every night of his exile for any sign.

Roh levered himself stiffly out from amongst the rocks, raising his head incrementally above the line of the outcrop to scan the shoreline in both directions. He had learnt the hard way, having been set upon by roaming bands of thieves enough times out here, and had sometimes been forced to remain hidden in whatever crack or crevice he found himself for days at a time until the pickings from the rockpools grew thin, and the creatures – most often young male Commoners – moved on. Today the stretch of colourstone beach was empty, and Roh clambered out onto the sand, his toes sinking into swirls of crimson and yellow.

The sun hung low in the west, fat and pink and scorching. Across the gleaming sands small creatures scuttled, their shadows tapering: fish clothed in ornate, transparent shells filled with water, only their tufted limbs poking out beneath; scaly mammals that lumbered past, dragging a groove in the sand behind them, their possessions heaped upon their backs. Flying

Eloths, flapping with the webbed skin of their fingers, dipped and dove, snapping up the creatures of the shore before they could dash between the safety of the rockpools. A flock settled to munch on their prizes, salt water pouring from cracked-open shells, each turning one bright crimson eye on Roh as he shuffled past.

He trudged to the water's edge, the waves lapping over his feet, and bent to wash his face. The seawater stung his ruined skin, snapping him awake at last. Along the shore he could make out a forest of strange forms standing in the evening haze. He would be there by nightfall, he supposed, continuing his wanderings by the light of the moon.

Roh wetted a finger and stuffed it into his mouth, polishing his stumpy teeth until they squeaked. The sores and ulcers on his gums began to bleed at once, and he spat into the water, watching dispassionately as creatures swirled up from the sand to taste his juices. A brightly painted mollusc, rolling along on a wheel of shell, came darting by, siphoning up a gust of the red-stained water and speeding off into the depths as the next wave came sliding in. Roh swallowed, his mouth thick with salt, and continued on his way.

A track of footprints seemed to end further up the beach, towards the towering, bleached forest; it was as if their maker had vanished into thin air. Roh paused, peering, having learnt the signs. At the point where the footprints stopped the sand was particularly shiny and slightly humped, as if something lay beneath. As Roh watched it shifted minutely, a bubble rising on the glossy surface: enough to tell him that a large predator – only the fingers of which he'd ever seen – dwelt beneath, waiting. The abruptly terminated footprints of its last victim always gave it away.

Roh stepped around it, the enigmatic forest, the details of which he still couldn't quite make out, looming closer. Its trees were pale and stationary – unusual in a world where the plantlife often had a mind and hunger of its own – and towered, curling, over one another. Roh crept on, keeping low to the sand, his bag dragging, until he realised. Bones. It was a forest of bones – a great sea creature washed ashore. A fire had been lit at its heart, casting the shadows of the great ribs long around it. Things slouched around the light, their forms crouched over the flame as they turned a spit, and Roh gave the scene a wide berth. They looked like Tallfolk, but of a different breed than any he'd seen, even out here.

Beyond, the shoreline seemed to glow. Sometimes the bandit kings, at war with one another in perpetuity, set fire to the flammable beaches of colourstone. Roh had no choice but to carry on, for he had pledged his allegiance to Enzeh, de-facto ruler of these parts, and only at Enzeh's fort could he find a semblance of safety from whatever had marked the sand around his camp.

He followed the rising moon, yellow in the twilight, a lone figure trudging the endless shore.

The dreams, back again. The looming of a shadow he couldn't understand.

Roh snapped awake, flailing his arms, staggering and almost falling. He gazed into the darkness, rummaging for his lantern and lighting it with trembling hands, a pebble of colourstone flaming and smoking in its base.

Something was different. He swung the lantern higher.

Something marked the sand at the edge of his light. Roh peered, eyes swivelling to scan the empty rockpools, moving past pristine sand to the scrawl of pattern drawn in the shore. It was back.

Hurry, his unravelled mind whimpered as he packed his belongings and lurched into the darkness. Roh made to extinguish his lamp, but in his fumbling dropped it instead. It shattered, pouring a blob of slowly spreading liquid flame across the sand, lighting up the night behind him.

He hadn't told them he was coming, and he hadn't told them what he was running from. Roh hadn't even met king Enzeh, only his flunkies, who'd come to demand a beach tax when word of a new hermit had reached their ears; he could only hope their promises of protection still stood.

Roh ran until the sun rose, his breath heaving and gulping from his lips, bag swinging back and forth, back and forth, sawing into the sun-ruined flesh of his neck. At sunup he collapsed, gasping, locking his legs just in time before he fell flat on his face. The morning light seemed to dim and flicker at the corners of his vision, and then he risked his first look back.

Nothing. Just the haze of distance and never-ending sand. Roh gazed into the shimmering heat, waiting. It was another Twicenight to the fort, he guessed, though he had never been there himself. Perhaps there was no fort, no *king Enzeh*, and he'd been conned, as he had at first suspected.

Roh allowed himself a glance ahead again. In the darkness he had followed the shore, heading for the glow in the distance. Now it was light, and the fires were a far, tawny smudge of smoke, rising to blend with the blue. He took a breathless, dribbling drink of bitter water – liberated from the bladder of a wanderfish – and lurched to a stand once more, his jog resumed.

The Long Stretch. Roh had heard of it from a chatty thief he'd met in a cave, not quite believing. But here it was, blazing ahead of him in the midday heat, a swathe of beach unbroken to the shimmering horizon.

His lungs were burning, his muscles ravaged by a day and night on the move, his bile water long since finished. If he didn't stop now he would collapse and die.

Roh looked back across the distance, still unable to see any sign of life, and creaked to a squat, his joints snapping. He hurled his woolen cloak over his head, suddenly dripping sweat in the hot darkness. He had a last bulb of fresh water in his pocket, and drank it off in one gulp. No food but the dried skin of a Gripf, which he'd been using as a seal for the bottom of his ripped pack. He peeled it carefully away and chewed on the crispy skin. He couldn't go on like this for much longer. Roh swallowed, the crisped shreds of skin scratching his throat on the way down. Perhaps death would be for the best. He had served his punishment.

He must have slept for a time, squatting and baking beneath his ripped cloak, the sweat simmering on his skin, and when Roh awoke he was desperate with thirst. He threw the cloak off to limp to the water, the sun still hammering down.

He found a wheeled Roller mollusc and crushed it with his fist, squeezing the thing above his open mouth until some yellow liquid came dripping out. Roh ate the rest raw, munching as he surveyed the liquid haze of the shore. His mouth paused, mid-chew.

There was something following him, wavering in the heat. He peered, shading his eyes with the flat of a hand, unable to quite make it out. But beside it, walking alongside, were the squat, unmistakable blobs of Commoners and Strongfolk.

Roh dropped the remainder of his supper and groaned to his feet, breath huffing quickly in his ears. He ran.

Night. Moonless and cloudy and so dark that Roh couldn't see the hand he held before his eyes. But he could see the lights of a dwelling larger than any hovel, perched on what must have been an outcrop above the shore.

He had heard them all day, voices, drifting from behind. Those same wobbling shapes in the shimmer, spread out and walking. Roh had run as if through flowing water, his legs fighting an unseen current of exhaustion, the sand constantly caving in beneath his blistered feet.

But here he was at last, the light of the fort drenching the sands. Roh waved his arms and cried out in croaking sobs, his spots flashing. The fort seemed to watch, impassive, unanswering. He crawled up the dunes, knowing they could shoot him at any moment, not caring. Soon he was up at the base of the wall, his breath wheezing, the darkness pressing at his back, fingers scrabbling along the wood for a gate of any kind, the long grass whispering around his chin.

He found it, open and unguarded, and a flicker of fresh terror surfaced. Roh pushed it open and fell inside, slamming the gate behind him.

Colourstone lanterns blazed, smoking, along the walls. *Where was everyone?*

Roh piled a few sleeping staffs, a cauldron and some Tallfolk chairs against the door, then wandered further in, heart drumming, legs weak.

The place looked to have been left in a hurry. The baking embers of a fire still glowed in a pit, surrounded by leaning staffs. Food littered the floor, and Roh hurriedly scooped what he could into his mouth before moving on, tasting the grit of the floor and taking the steps to an upper level that must look out over the coast in all directions.

He came up to a viewing platform, roofed over and cut with oval windows. A few dropped paddlestones clinked under his feet, the single lantern illuminating the bare walls of the empty place, their timbers scrawled with messy spot colour graffiti and old, dried stains.

Roh peeped out of one of the windows, seeing nothing but darkness outside. The waves breathed in a hushed sigh below. He pressed his eye to the next window, surveying the black nothingness to the west, then moved to the side wall, gazing off towards what would have been a wasteland of Slaughterwoods, creeks and hills that terminated at the nearest country border, a great mote as wide as the mightiest river and guarded at every crossing. He could not go that way, into the darkness. Finally Roh turned his gaze east, into yet more black, to an unknown world beyond the fort. The beach continued all around the Everywhere, surrounding it. He supposed if he ran far enough he'd just end up right back here, forever afraid of the patient walkers in the haze.

Roh turned his ear to the northerly window, listening for any sound from the shore. Only the waves, and a hooting cry of something small, drifted from that darkness. Would the soldiers of the underworld, hired from hardened guilds and liberated from prisons, really fear the lights of this fort? Roh wondered what other gates to the place must be standing open to the night, and shut the trapdoor in the floor of the lookout tower. He still had his paddle, his spear, and he squatted in the corner, weapons brandished, waiting, eyelids heavier than they'd ever been before.

A dry, smoked scent, like old, burnt leaves. Roh's nose twitched as he opened his eyes.

Darkness, still. But the moon had risen beyond the window, a crescent of yellow.

The crescent shifted, and Roh's eyes focused. Now the moon was full.

How...?

Something came between him and the moonlight again, and Roh drew a sharp hiss of breath.

He fixed the darkness with an unblinking, frozen stare, and saw its eyes shine in return: a glimmer of reflected moonlight.

'Found you,' said a rasping voice to his side, startling Roh so that he screamed aloud, spots flaring at the same time.

The old Commoner, Vhis, moved forward into the moonlight.

Roh spared him only a glance, his gaze drawn back to the shadow before him. He groped for the paddle weapon, but it was nowhere in reach. Outside, muffled voices drifted from below the walls, waiting. He remembered his spear, tucked behind his back against the wall. Roh pulled it out and brandished it before the thing, the shaft glowing in the light of the moon, its fossil tip lost in shadow.

The Commoner hissed, lumbering to grasp the shaft of Roh's spear. Roh blazed his spots and pushed with all his might towards the shadow, falling forwards and bracing his legs. The shadow, painted in stipples of colour from Roh's spots, swept to one side, a sickening stretch of limb revealed suddenly in the shaft of light, that burnt stink intensifying, the spear jabbing past it into empty space. Vhis wrenched it out of Roh's grasp at last and stood between him and the shadow, filling his view.

Roh squeezed his eyes shut, ready for the end. He heard the spear being dragged away. Then moonlight lit up his eyelids. Vhis had moved aside.

Roh opened his eyes. The thing had come forward into the light, and his mind reeled at the sight of it, the foreign make of its design; an apparition surely made somewhere else, far away.

But its attention was fixed on the spear, and it clutched the fossil blade in something that was as far from a hand as Roh could imagine, snapping it deftly free. Roh and the Commoner watched, motionless, as the thing brought the piece of fossilized leaf to its face, examining it closely from every conceivable angle.

It spoke then, in a bubbling, rippling voice like something thicker than water gurgling from a spout. Just a single word, perhaps, four sounds strung loosely together. To Roh it sounded like *Hhen-Rhi-Ehh-Tah.*

Vhis flickered a pattern of incredulity: *really?* The thing turned to him, shadows enclosing its form once more, the expression on its madness-inducing head seeming to change. It held up the fossil, stabbing the dark air for emphasis, and Vhis beamed, his spots deluging them all with light. Roh caught a pastel-tinted view of its entire body, and felt his last meal rising in his gullet.

Vhis went to the window that overlooked the beach, shouting a word in Tall that Roh didn't know. He looked to see the line of rag-tag hunters dispersing, tramping back the way they'd come, long shadows receding in the moonlight. The Commoner himself, without so much as another word or a look back at Roh, opened the hatch in the floor and climbed down, out of sight.

Roh felt himself trembling uncontrollably, faced with the vision of another world still crouching before him, filling the observation tower. It licked the surface of its prize, roughness rasping against the minute, hair-fine mineral ridges of the pattern, and then rose with one great liquid movement, standing stooped under the ceiling, gazing down at Roh.

He met the shine of its eyes once more, seeing viscous, churning currents pulse and ebb beneath their translucent skins, and then it folded itself neatly into the aperture of the hatch in the floor, and was gone.

Epilogue

Record of reserved spot sheets, copied at great expense. Dialogue with Emai Bhur Jahm, held at Puriel-Centre.

Interviewer, analytics guild-member Sumht: Emai Bhur Jahm... *(reads)* prisoner considered for release, my congratulations.

Jahm: Yes. Thank you.

Sumht: On the condition that you tell us all you know regarding what transpired at Lake Oph.

Jahm: *(Tuts his assent)*.

Sumht: You were... you *met* the instigator of this crime, yes?

Jahm: Of course. I was an employee, I suppose you'd say.

Sumht: In return for what? The Gleam?

Jahm: Yes. Precisely. Powdered Flashstone and Heavy Viimt, mostly, still present in great abundance inside the bones of the Oph beasts.

Sumht: And your... employer? What did he... *it* stand to gain?

Jahm: It was after something meaningless to us, as far as anyone in the organisation could tell. A treasure, a technology. Dropped somewhere and lost.

Sumht: What treasure? Expand.

Jahm: *(Exhales)*. The way it was described to us... Long, long ago, the Oph beasts presided over the Everywhere, yes? They had mastered flight, and travelled further, *much* further, than we guessed. They even went to the neighbouring star – the one we call Zulahmm. *(Pause)*. And they found creatures there. Thinking beings, like us. Like them. But it was not a happy meeting, and the Oph beasts stole from them. They took something unique, it was said, something nobody else had ever thought of making before, and could never make again.

Sumht: What?

Jahm: I have no idea. It didn't deign to tell us, did it? Maybe – *probably* – we wouldn't understand if it had. All we knew was that the Oph beasts went there long ago and fought their neighbours, stealing this thing from them. But there was a chase, it seemed, and they lost it on the way home. Between the stars.

Sumht: *(Long pause)*. This all pertains to the fossils, how?

Jahm: Because the Oph beasts kept a *record* of the location, the place where it was lost. In their puzzle machines. Their World Brain, as it was described to us. *(Pause)*. My employer said the cloud of stars we live in turns, like a Roller's foot, very slowly. And a whole turn of the cloud has brought us back near to the place where this thing was dropped. It got what it needed, I assume. Vanished thirteen seasons ago and never came back.

Sumht: Leaving the Kirha Organisation high and dry. Not very nice.

Jahm: Hmm. We hoped it would come back, someday.

Sumht: I'm sure. Well I can tell you that nothing else like the object – the... *World Brain* – you describe was found in the Oph haul at Ophiphi, or at the other site in Daum, discovered in the same strata. How could this be?

Jahm: I don't know.

Sumht: You don't know?

Jahm: What do I have to lose? Old Vhis is dead, the Organisation is dissolved; I am immune. Why would I lie?

Sumht: That remains to be seen. There is no visual record

of this thing you speak of, only its description. A complex pattern of stone, the size of a finger claw, yes?

Jahm: That's right.

Sumht: Fine. *(Spot pages shuffling)*. And what became of the convict who gave this treasure away? Emai Icai Roh? You never returned for your vengeance?

Jahm: *(A flash of spots)*.

Sumht: I indicate for the pages that the Bhur Jahm has shrugged.

A figure, stooped and plodding, its long shadow bristled with tapering whiskers, walked the vastness of the shore.

Thirteen seasons, and he had come full circle. The fort stood above the beach, much as he remembered it, but burnt out, blackened. Roh dumped his things in the mirrorgrass, locking his aching limbs and staring out to sea while he stroked the rough spines around his jaw, red now with age.

Back again, but now with one less foot and a few more scars, the whole continent having revolved beneath his limping stride. He would stay here for the Twicenight, he supposed, cook his catch and watch the turning of the heavens as darkness fell. Then perhaps he would move on, all the way around once more. He might even make it back here before he died. Roh thought little about the past anymore, and why he had come to be where he was; above him glowed ten thousand worlds, the haunt of whatever had come to him that night, only to vanish into the darkness. It was the future, held suspended amongst that luminous vault of stars, that fascinated him now.

About the Author

Tom Toner was born in Somerset in 1986. He is the author of *The Promise of the Child* (2015), *The Weight of the World* (2017) and *The Tropic of Eternity* (2018), all published by Gollancz, which together form the 147th century space opera series The Amaranthine Spectrum.

NewCon Press Novellas Set 7: Robot Dreams

What do robots dream of? Inspired by Fangorn's wonderful artwork, four of our finest science fiction authors determine to provide an answer in four stand-alone novellas.

Andrew Bannister introduces us to Kovac, an agent of the Mandate, assigned to a world whose inhabitants have no idea that they are an experiment. Kovac begins to realise there are agencies at work that have no place being there…

Ren Warom guides us through the lives of Niner, from soldier to body double to killer to scrap yard attendant. Niner only functions due to a malfunction that goes undetected, baffling its creators when they fail to duplicate their success.

Justina Robson shows us the rise of A.I., through subtle infiltration and more brazen manipulation, from gentle persuasion to blatant coercion, until the world is no longer ours. All for our own good, of course.

Tom Toner takes us to a primitive world where a bomb fell aeons ago, a world whose people will risk anything, even the monsters said to haunt the shores of Lake Oph, to mine the priceless substance known as *Gleam*…

www.newconpress.co.uk

IMMANION PRESS

Purveyors of Speculative Fiction

Breathe, My Shadow by Storm Constantine

A standalone Wraeththu Mythos novel. Seladris believes he carries a curse making him a danger to any who know him. Now a new job brings him to Ferelithia, the town known as the Pearl of Almagabra. But Ferelithia conceals a dark past, which is leaking into the present. In the strange old house, Inglefey, Seladris tries to deal with hauntings of his own and his new environment, until fate leads him to the cottage on the shore where the shaman Meladriel works his magic. Has Seladris been drawn to Ferelithia to help Meladriel repel a malevolent present or is he simply part of the evil that now threatens the town? ISBN: 978-1-912815-06-7 £13.99, $17.99 pbk

The Lord of the Looking Glass by Fiona McGavin

The author has an extraordinary talent for taking genre tropes and turning them around into something completely new, playing deftly with topsy-turvy relationships between supernatural creatures and people of the real world. 'Post Garden Centre Blues' reveals an unusual relationship between taker and taken in a twist of the changeling myth. 'A Tale from the End of the World' takes the reader into her developing mythos of a post-apocalyptic world, which is bizarre, Gothic and steampunk all at once. Following in the tradition of exemplary short story writers like Tanith Lee and Liz Williams, Fiona has a vivid style of writing that brings intriguing new visions to fantasy, horror and science fiction. ISBN: 978-1-907737-99-2, £11.99, $17.50 pbk

The Heart of the Moon by Tanith Lee

Clirando, a celebrated warrior, believes herself to be cursed. Betrayed by people she trusted, she unleashes a vicious retaliation upon them and then lives in fear of fateful retribution for her act of cold-blooded vengeance. Set in a land resembling Ancient Greece, in this novella Tanith Lee explores the dark corners of the heart and soul within a vivid mythical adventure. The book also includes 'The Dry Season' another of her tales set in an imaginary ancient world of the Classical era.

ISBN: 978-1-912815-05-0 £10.99, $14.99 pbk

www.immanion-press.com
info@immanion-press.com

www.ingramcontent.com/pod-product-compliance
Lightning Source LLC
Chambersburg PA
CBHW020824150626
46554CB00018B/2330

9 781912 950553